You're a hero, Peerie Bear!

You're a hero, Peerie Bear!
Written by Gillian Fox.
Illustrated by Eve Eunson.

ISBN 0-9536190-0-1

Published by Another Cat-astrophe!
Skeotaing, Clousta,
Shetland.
ZE2 9LX
01595 810461

Printed by Shetland Litho, Gremista, Lerwick.

You're a hero, Peerie Bear!

Written by Gillian Fox
Illustrated by Eve Eunson

This book is dedicated to the crews and familes of the Shetland lifeboats, and all those who risk their lives for ours.

PEERIE Bear was not having one of his best days. Jess's cousins from the city had come to stay with Granny and Granpa for the school holidays, and he, for one, would not be sorry when they went home. Jessie had spent almost the whole holiday ignoring him, and while he knew she often got lonely on their tiny island, he really didn't think it was quite fair to be left in her toy chest the whole day.

It was different when bedtime came though, oh yes, he was soon pulled out then. He had considered hiding one night, to teach Jess a lesson, but the thought of spending the whole night in the dark with a stuffed giraffe who snored and a clockwork ballerina who never stopped moaning about "how she could have been a star" would have driven him clean out of his fur.

He had hoped today would be a little better, but it wasn't looking that way so far. Taking matters into his own paws, he had crept into Jessie's backpack when she wasn't looking, and hidden among the sandwiches Mum had packed for their picnic. He would have an exciting day if it was the last thing he did. He hadn't seen much excitement this holiday, and as Cameron and Jamie would be leaving tomorrow to go back to school, this might be his last chance.

He was muttering to himself about out what a bad lot his life was, when the flap of the rucksack opened and Jess peered in. As he squinted into the sun, she lifted him out and sat him on the grass among them.

"Peerie Bear, you wee rascal, you should be at home," smiled Jess. Peerie Bear smiled back. He knew Jess wouldn't really have left him behind, she just needed reminding now and then.

After lunch, Jessie decided that she would show her cousins the seal pups that gathered along the foot of the rocky cliff, waiting for their mothers to return from catching fish out at sea. Peerie Bear didn't like the sound of that at all. He knew that although selkie pups looked very cute, they had a nasty bite if you went too near. Reminding Jess to be careful, he lay back against her jacket and dozed in the sun, very pleased with himself for arranging this lovely day out.

Peerie Bear suddenly felt strange, and opened his eyes to find he was being watched very closely by a fearsome looking bird.

"You gluffed me clean out of my wits!" yelled Peerie Bear, "Don't you know it's rude to stare at folk, especially when they are sleeping!"

"Sorry, sorry, sorry!" squawked the seagull. "Out hunting. Thought say hello. Well, not hunting. What tell wife. In bad book. No fish. Not my fault. Keeping out way. Bad bad temper!"

Peerie Bear had never heard such a din in his life.

"Can't you speak quietly? I might be stuffed but I'm not deaf!" yelled Peerie Bear above the racket.

"Sorry, sorr …"

"Stop! Not that again. Now lets start from the beginning. I'm Peerie Bear from the croft over the hill. What's your name?"

"O'Maalie!" shrieked the gull, flapping his wings loudly, as he stalked around Peerie Bear with his head to one side.

"Stop doing that, it makes me nervous!" said bear. O'Maalie settled himself down and began to preen his feathers. Suddenly he stopped, and thrust his head towards Peerie Bear, who almost fell over backwards in fright.

"Like eyes!" he screeched.

"Well, thank you, that's very kind, but actually one of them isn't mine, it's a button Grannie stitched on. I don't know where the real one went, but I have always had a good idea," he said, thinking back to the day the dog had looked guilty for hours.

"No! Like eyes. Want eyes. Shiny. Wife like! O'Maalie in best books take eyes!"

"Hang on a minute!" screamed Peerie Bear putting his paws over his face, "You can't have my eyes. I need them!"

"Humpff!" muttered O'Maalie, "In bad books now!" and he stalked off to the edge of the cliff and gazed out to sea, trying to look very wise.

Several hours passed, and O'Maalie sat on the cliff, peering around occasionally and muttering to himself in birdspeak about unfriendly bears.

Peerie Bear realised that the sun had passed way overhead and was setting over the hill. He knew that meant it would be dark soon, and that Jess and the boys should have been back a long time ago. He began to get very worried.

Peerie Bear coughed loudly.

O'Maalie rotated his head in a way that made Peerie Bear squirm. He remembered Jess doing that to him once and it wasn't nice!

"What, what, what? You give eyes now! Good, good, in best books now!"

"Er, well no, not exactly …" replied Peerie Bear, feeling quite embarrassed, "I wondered if you would do me a favour? I'm worried about Jess and the boys, and I'd be very grateful if you would fly down and have a look?"

O'Maalie squawked and flapped his wings, "Busy, busy, busy. Hunting. Wife angry. No time!"

Then Peerie Bear had a magnificent idea!

"I'll give you eyes, I mean, not my eyes, 'cos I need them, but I know where Grannie keeps the spare ones, lots of them. You could take them to your wife!"

"Yes, yes!" squealed O'Maalie in excitement, "You friend bear! O'Maalie go now!" and with a flurry of white he launched himself into the air and soared high above the cliff top.

O'Maalie looked down, scouring the beach and cliffs for Jess and her cousins. Suddenly he saw them stranded on the rocks where the tide and come in and cut them off from the beach. Screaming loudly, he landed next to Peerie Bear and told him how he had found the children and the danger they were in.

"We must fetch help!" Looking out to sea, Peerie Bear saw a fishing boat. "Fly out and attract their attention!"

O'Maalie did not need telling twice. This was the most exciting day he could ever remember! Grasping Jess's jacket in his powerful beak, he set off towards the boat, and dropped it on the deck by the feet of the fishermen.

Screeching and screaming, he circled the boat, until they had no choice but to follow his path towards the shore.

Cameron saw the boat in the distance, and soon all three bairns were waving and shouting for help.

Within a few minutes, they heard the loud rumble of the lifeboat approaching, and tired, cold and wet, they were taken aboard to safety.

"Jessie Baxter! I'm surprised at you," said the coxswain of the lifeboat sternly.

"You know how dangerous it is to climb down cliffs, especially without an adult around!"

Jessie looked very sheepish, and realised she and her cousins had had a very lucky escape indeed!

The following day, a reporter from *The Shetland Times* came to take a photo of the three bairns, and Jess excitedly explained to him that it was thanks to Peerie Bear and his friend O'Maalie that they had been rescued.

"Yes, dear!" he said patting her on the head.

A talking bear! And as for seagulls! Everyone knew how stupid they were!

He lined up the children and the crew of the lifeboat for a picture. Rubbing his eyes, he looked through the viewfinder again. He must have had one too many glasses of Granpa Baxters' parsnip wine. He could have sworn the teddy bear and the strange looking gull sitting on the fence were winking at him!

But they couldn't be. Could they?

By the same author

    Peerie Bear & the Fire Festival

Forthcoming Titles

    Peerie Bear's new Friend
    Peerie Bear & The Trow
    Peerie Bear Rides Again
    Peerie Bear meets Oscar Charlie